THE BABY-SITTERS CLUB®

THE OFFICIAL COLORING BOOK

BASED ON THE BESTSELLING SERIES BY
ANN M. MARTIN

ART BY FRAN BRYLEWSKA FOR ARTFUL DOODLERS

SCHOLASTIC INC.

T0026086

ISBN 978-1-338-89241-3

10 9 8 7 6 5 4 3 2 1   23 24 25 26 27
Printed in the U.S.A.   40
First printing 2023

Compiled by Jenna Ballard
Art by Fran Brylewska for Artful Doodlers

JENNY PREZZIOSO

NEW JERSEY

JESSI RAMSEY
JUNIOR OFFICER

JACKIE RODOWSKY

ASHLEY
WYETH

LOGAN BRUNO
ASSOCIATE MEMBER

LOGAN LIKES

MARY ANNE!

SHANNON KILBOURNE
ASSOCIATE MEMBER

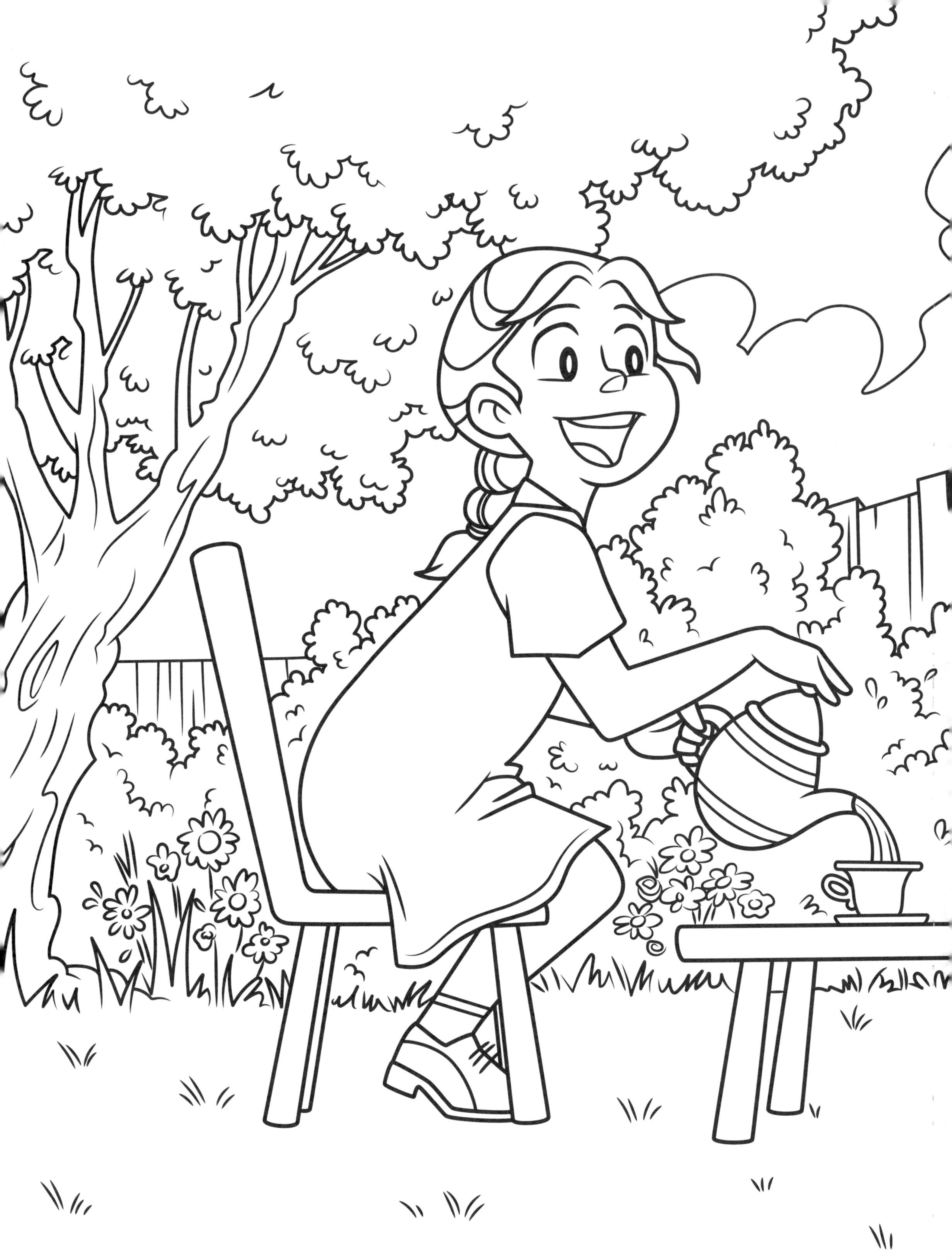

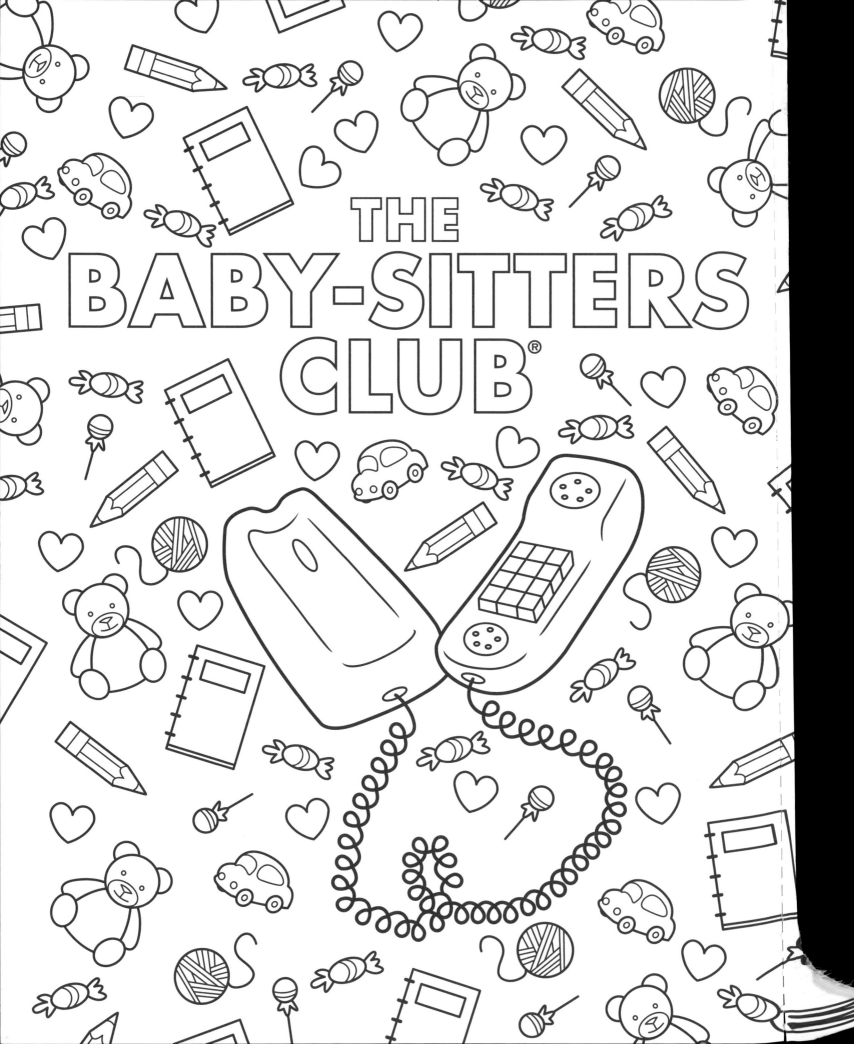

THE BABY-SITTERS CLUB®